What's in a Name?

A Story about George Eliot

Story by Michelle Atkins
Illustrations by Loma Tilders

Marian Evans (George Eliot)
1819-1880

Mary Ann Evans was born in England and grew up in an era that is often considered old-fashioned today. Hard work was valued, and society rules were strict. Women were mostly expected to stay at home and raise a family. But, unlike many women of her time, Mary Ann was educated and became known for her strong intellect.

Mary Ann moved to London and worked as an assistant editor for a magazine. She changed her name to Marian and wrote articles and book reviews. At age 37, Marian began writing fiction, under the name *George Eliot*. She met George Henry Lewes, possibly her greatest friend, around this time.

During her lifetime, Marian *George Eliot* Evans was considered one of the world's greatest novelists. She died at the age of 61.

Novels by George Eliot:
Adam Bede (1859)
The Mill on the Floss (1860)
Silas Marner (1861)
Middlemarch (1871)
Daniel Deronda (1876)

Contents

Chapter 1

The Secret

My name is George Eliot... and Marian Evans. As an author, I am a man, but in real life, I am a woman. Not many people know this, so you must promise to keep it a secret.

As George Eliot, I am famous. As Marian Evans, I do not have many friends. My life is one of contrasts.

If you met me at my home in England, you would simply see a 40-year-old woman. You would probably find me plain to look at, but interesting to talk with. If you talked to some of my neighbors, you might even hear some unpleasant gossip about me and how I live.

You see, I am not exactly "normal" for a woman of my time. I do not have many friends. I do not belong to the gardening club or anything like that. I do not have children. I am not even married. In fact, if it weren't for my great friend, George Henry Lewes, I would almost be alone in the world.

Chapter 2

A Woman's Work

Our society tells me that, as a woman, I cannot do and cannot be certain things. I am told that my proper place in the world is at home. If I want to work, then I must work at home, and only after all the household chores are done.

I find these chores dreary and boring. I have always wanted more from life. I enjoy learning, reading, and writing—more than most people realize. You see, I am a published writer.

Writing is one thing that I can do at home to use my brain. When I am writing, I feel free. Well, almost. Because I am a woman, there are still some things I cannot write about if I want to be published. As a normal woman, I would be expected to write about issues such as ladies' manners and household topics.

I knew that being a female writer would be difficult. I had already seen the fate of my female writing peers, some of whom had been published, all of whom had been harshly received due to their "female" writing.

But, to date, I have managed to be very productive on a range of topics. As a writer, I have pretended to be a man.

Chapter 3

The False Name

I created the false name of George Eliot. ("George" being the name of my friend to whom I introduced you earlier, and "Eliot" because it is easy to pronounce.)

As George Eliot, I can channel all my knowledge into my stories. As George Eliot, I am not afraid that, if I write about certain subjects, they will be rejected as being unacceptable coming from a woman. As George Eliot, I can just be myself.

So, you see, the false name of George Eliot is very precious to me. It protects me. You can imagine therefore, how disturbed I was when the following letter came to me, through the care of my publisher. (My publisher had recognized my handwriting on a manuscript and guessed my true identity only months ago. Just like me, he was committed to keeping my secret.)

Chapter 4

The Letter

January 2, 1859

Dear Mr. Eliot,

Allow me to introduce myself. My name is Arthur Willows. I am an artist who likes to paint people held in high regard by society. I have read your novel **Adam Bede**, and I would be honored to paint your portrait.

You have the reputation of being the most gifted novelist to have emerged in recent times. Please send me a letter at the provided address to let me know if you are interested in my proposal. I imagine that the completed portrait would take about three to four weeks of regular sittings.

Subject to your consent, I would also like to include your portrait in an exhibition called "Important Writers of the 19th Century." This exhibition is being held on March 2, 1859, at the National Portrait Gallery in London.

I look forward to hearing from you.

Yours truly,

Arthur Willows

Chapter 5

The Decision

My hands were shaking when I finished reading this letter, from both excitement and fear. What was I to do? I had managed to keep my secret from everyone except my publisher and a few chosen, close friends. There were rumors, of course; one being that George Eliot was a clergyman!

I couldn't risk being identified. But I didn't want to pass up this valuable opportunity.

After much consideration, I decided that I would go ahead with the project. I would simply dress up as a man! I would borrow my friend George's clothes and arrange for him to find me a false beard from one of his theater friends. I would tuck my hair under a wig and hat. I would practice how to walk, stand, and sit like a man. I already had a deep voice, so I could strengthen this. I was going to do it! I was actually going to become George Eliot!

Within days of receiving his letter, I wrote back to Mr. Willows and accepted his proposal.

Chapter 6

The Disguise

At last the day arrived. I was ready. I had practiced my disguise many times. I was quite comfortable in my new clothes. I wore a black suit, white shirt, and a pin-striped waistcoat. My hair was fixed back neatly so that I could wear the wig and the beard. The beard was very itchy, but I needed to cover up my whiskerless skin! Unfortunately, I could not pass as a young man with no facial hair, because I had the wrinkles of a 40-year-old!

George could only get me a black wig. The wig did not match my general skin coloring and eyebrows, but I did not think this was too much of a problem. However, I was afraid of loose hairs escaping from under my wig, so I wore a black hat to weigh it down on my head.

I had also studied the walking, sitting, and general body language of my friend George, so I was quite confident when, at last, Mr. Willows knocked at my door.

Mr. Willows was very charming when he met me. He assured me that he would keep our arrangement secret. Mr. Willows complimented my writing and said he was honored to be able to paint me. I felt flattered and started to relax during the first portrait session.

There were some nervous moments when Mr. Willows asked about my background. He asked me how I had developed into a writer and where I had been educated. I pretended to be embarrassed by his attention so that soon he stopped asking me questions. In fact, by the end of the first session, Mr. Willows thought I was a shy and anti-social gentleman.

"I hope it is not too forward of me, Mr. Eliot, but your public personality is very different from the bold narrator whom I have met in your books," he said.

However, when Mr. Willows talked about interesting topics of conversation, such as philosophy or history, I found the "shy act" very hard to perform. But I had to speak as little as possible because I knew that I was not able to sustain a deep male voice for long stretches of time.

I realize that my shyness made Mr. Willows' job very difficult for him. An artist needs to engage his or her subject in conversation to get to know them, and to then transfer this personal insight onto the canvas. If Mr. Willows had known the truth, he would have been totally confused, and may have painted a large, red question mark on his fresh white canvas!

Chapter 7

The Fateful Day

Everything was going smoothly with Mr. Willows until the fourth sitting. This was the sitting when he started to apply detailed work on my face. This was the sitting when the disaster happened.

"Mr. Eliot," said Mr. Willows, "I feel that your handsome face is being hidden by the shadow of your hat. I know that we agreed to include the hat because it looked stately, but I would like to see you without it."

It was at this stage that Mr. Willows suddenly leaped over to me and whisked off my hat—and my wig—without even giving me a moment to react! One moment I was sitting quietly on my seat in the right pose, and the next I was scrambling noisily for my wig, which had flopped to the floor.

And then there was silence. Mr. Willows looked at me—straight at me—and his mouth dropped open.

"Mr. Eliot, I do apologize! I had no idea that you wore a wig. Please forgive my insensitivity. I have an uncle who cannot accept his baldness either, and who…"

And then he stopped very suddenly. His eyes moved over my full head of long, brown hair—hair which was of a very different color than my beard and which had loosened from its pins. I remember watching him watching me as he pieced together the startling situation, until at last he spoke.

"Mr. Eliot… who are you?"

Chapter 8

The Explanation

It was at this stage that I took a deep breath and tried to compose myself so I could tell Mr. Willows my story. I explained how I lived to write. I explained how honored I had felt when he had asked me to be his subject. I told him that I was frightened to disclose my real identity in case I was rejected, both as his portrait subject and as a serious writer.

I pleaded with him to understand that I had to create a male identity for my fiction writing. I asked him to understand that I could not risk the gossip about my being a woman tainting my fiction writing. I kept my voice level and strong, finishing my explanation with the following introduction.

"Mr. Willows. Allow me to introduce my other self. My name is Marian Evans. I write under the false name of George Eliot. I beg you—please help me to keep my secret... please."

Mr. Willows' eyes had remained large and alert throughout my whole speech. The silence seemed to go on forever. I could almost hear his eyes blink each time they registered another of my female features. He started with my hair, then my skin, then my neck and hands. He was quickly putting all the pieces of my identity puzzle together. I was very afraid of his response.

Suddenly, Mr. Willows moved away from me. Without saying a word, he took two large, heavy steps toward his easel and unclipped the partly-completed portrait. He leaned it against the wall with a sad thump.

Then he started to scrub the paint from his palette. He did this silently, his head bowed. It was as if I no longer existed. I did not take my eyes off him, watching as he removed the various traces of me from his artistic vision. I thought his face looked stern, but I could not read his expression. I willed him to speak... to say something... anything!

At last he spoke.

"Miss Evans. You are a fascinating and brave woman. I have a sister who spends her days and nights writing, only to have her work rejected by many publishers. They say her work is too strong and, therefore, unwomanly. I admire your courage. It really does not matter to me whether you are a woman or a man. You are an interesting person, and I would still like to paint your portrait."

"But please," he continued, "let me paint you as yourself—as Marian Evans. In time, you will no doubt be forced to reveal your true identity. Let us hope that you will be recognized for the impressive writer you are. And, only then, will I uncover my portrait. It will be the first portrait of you—Marian *George Eliot* Evans."

Chapter 9

The Clergyman

I remember that his words were spoken softly but firmly—and sweetly. I was on the verge of tears when my attention was distracted by the sound of heavy footsteps running toward us. Suddenly, the door was flung open and there was George. He was crimson in the face and puffing loudly. But then he noticed my loosened hair and turned momentarily silent.

"Mr. Eliot..." he said, looking deep into my eyes for some understanding, but then quickly continuing with a confused look on his face. "Mr. Eliot, Mr. Willows, I apologize to you both for the sudden interruption, but I need to talk with Mr. Eliot urgently... and privately."

"George, Mr. Willows knows who I am," I said, softly.

I will never forget George's expression as his eyes moved from me to Mr. Willows and then back to me. But he didn't waste a moment in reflection. George had something important to say.

"Marian, your publisher is in the drawing room. He has rushed over from town, where the debate about the identity of George Eliot has peaked. As you know, the most common view has been that George Eliot is a clergyman. In fact, one of the local pastors in town is pretending to be you! He has claimed your works as his own and is arguing that your publisher has not paid him for his writings. He is talking of suing your publisher, Marian! This has gone too far. You must reveal yourself!"

Chapter 10

The Plan

I looked at Mr. Willows. He was still. But then he moved toward us with a wide smile.

"Why, Miss Evans, and… and you, sir," he said, looking over at George. "I have a plan. As you know, the National Portrait Gallery is having an exhibition in a few weeks on important writers. I have not, as yet, informed them that I will be exhibiting George Eliot. But why don't we make a surprise appearance?"